To: the BOOKMIVEL

ALOHA BEAR

The Story of Aloha Bear™
ISLAND HERITAGE PUBLISHING
Copyright © 1986 Island Heritage Publishing
Fifth Printing—1991

Address orders and correspondence to:

ISLAND HERITAGE PUBLISHING
A division of The Madden Corporation
99-880 Iwaena Street
Aiea, Hawaii 96701
(808) 487-7299

ALOHA BEAR is a trademark of the Madden Corporation

Printed in Hong Kong

Published by

ISLAND HERITAGE

Written and Illustrated
by
Dick Adair

There was a stowaway
On Santa's sleigh
The night he left the pole.

A furry bear
In underwear
A warmer place his goal.

Hid among the toys
For girls and boys
Who live and play in the sun.

Went undiscovered
Until uncovered
When Santa's work
Was done.

"What do I see
Under that tree
Did I put that there?

Where on my list
Did I put this
A fuzzy polar bear?"

"Your eight reindeer
Brought me here
Though none of them really knew.

I sneaked my way
Aboard your sleigh
It was the only thing to do.

I was oh so lost
In that arctic frost
With all that snow and ice.

The nights so long
The temperature wrong
It really wasn't nice.

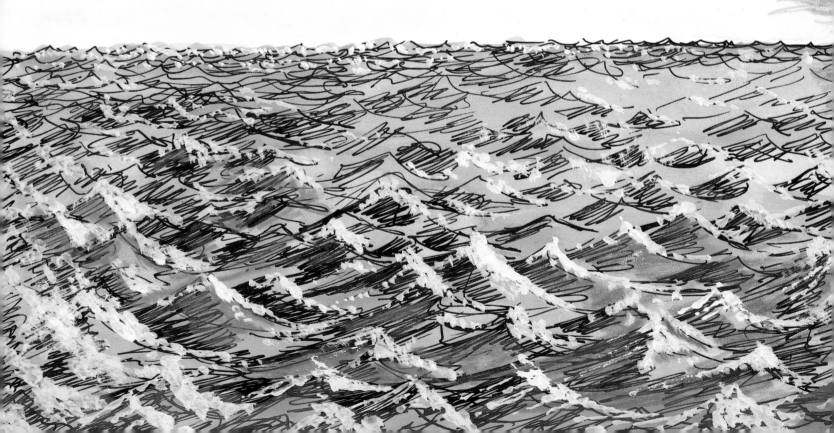

Though it's natural there
For a polar bear
I'm really not the norm.

I'd freeze all day
And never play
'Cause I never could get warm.

Then I saw your house
And crept like a mouse
Inside to thaw my nose.

There I discovered
An open cupboard
With bags of toys and clothes.

One I found
Marked: HAWAII BOUND
This was the one for me.

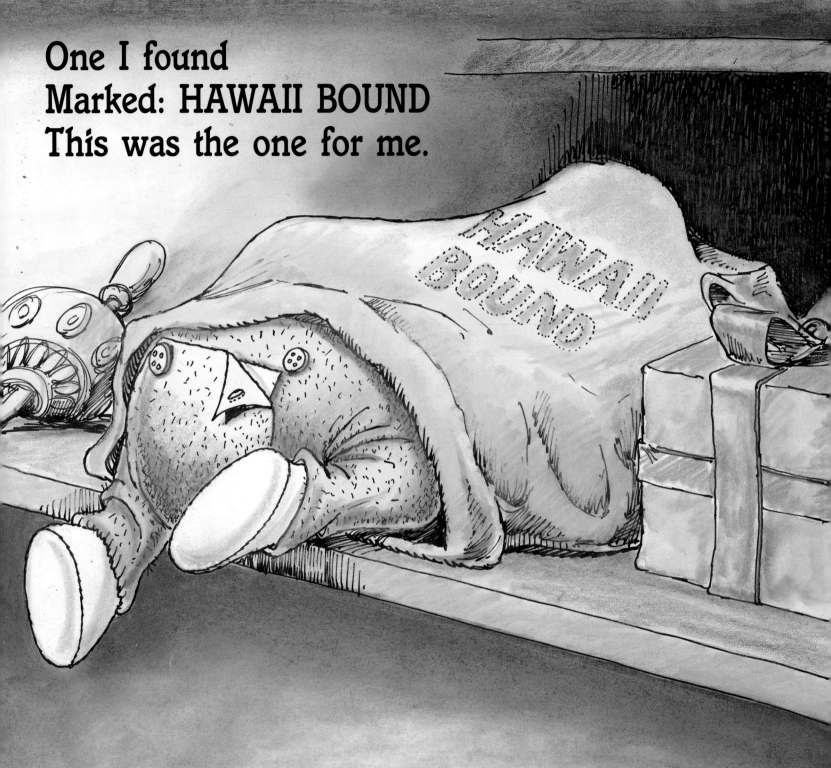

So I jumped inside
To wait my ride
To sunny sand and sea.

Now that you know
Please don't go
And take me
Far away.

I could never face
That cold cold place,
Oh please let me stay!"

With a twinkling smile
Santa sat a while
To figure this little bear's plight.

It was a grateful pause
For Santa Claus
It had been a very long winter's night.

Now try as he might
There was always some slight
Little gift not put on his sleigh.

For this last stop
His favorite spot
The land of Hawaii Nei.

Now this surprise
A cuddly prize
A wonderful gift to give.

"So don't despair
My little bear
Here is where you'll live.

My gift to you
Is a fond adieu
And some aloha clothes to wear.

And to thos
From fa
I giv
Aloh

ho come here
nd near
y
ear."

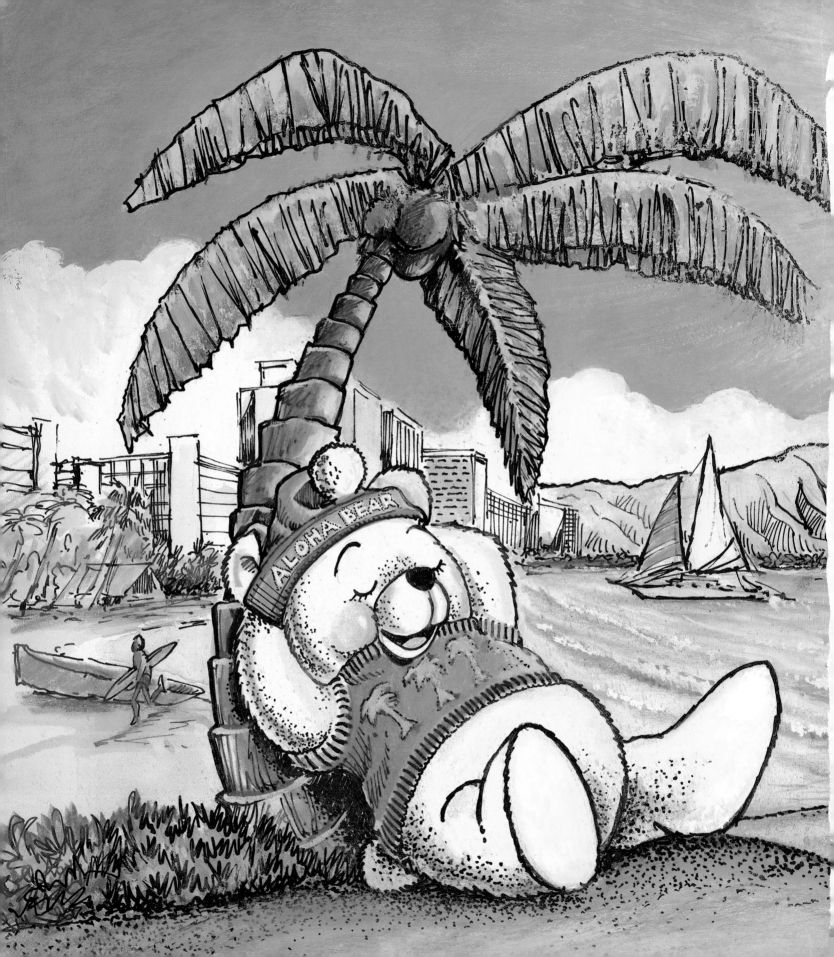